Dedicated to my Son, Nilan Varsani.

WHEN NILAN MET SANTA

Written by
Bhavna Varsani

Illustrations
Santhya Shenbagam R

It was a cold frosty morning. Nilan was excited. It was Christmas Eve. Nilan jumped out of bed and ran downstairs to check if he had any more presents under the Christmas tree.

Nilan couldn't see any new presents but dreamed of Santa coming down the chimney with a brand new blue shiny bike.

'Nilan. Are you ready?' called his mummy.
Nilan got ready to go shopping with his
mummy and daddy.

They were going to buy Christmas dinner.
Nilan loved shopping for Christmas dinner but
he especially looked forward to buying treats
for Santa and the reindeers. Every year Nilan
would help his mummy and daddy put out a
glass of milk with chocolate chip cookies and
juicy carrots for Santa's reindeers.

After dinner, it was almost bedtime so Nilan helped put the cookies, milk and carrots out near the chimney. Nilan switched the living room lights off and waited on the stairs to see if he could catch Santa leaving his present under the tree.

Nilan waited and waited..

and waited. But Santa didn't come

He fell asleep on the stairs.

Suddenly Nilan was woken up by a loud thud. 'It's Santa' he thought to himself. Nilan excitedly popped his head down to see if he could see Santa. To his surprise he could see two shiny black boots popping out of the chimney.

He then heard a deep voice
shouting 'Heeeeelp!' Santa was
stuck in the chimney.

Nilan quickly ran to the chimney and tried to pull Santa out but it was no good.

Santa's boots came flying off
and Nilan with them.

Nilan got back up and again tried to pull Santa down. This time he held Santa by the ankles and with all his strength gave a big hard pull.

It worked!

Finally, Nilan managed to help
Santa through the chimney.

santa, coughing said

'Here is your milk and cookies' Nilan said to Santa.

'And there are carrots for the reindeer', said Nilan.

'I didn't forget about them' he said proudly. 'Thank you' said Santa. 'But if I eat all of those cookies I will keep getting stuck in the chimney. Here is your christmas present' said Santa. Santa gurgled down the glass of cold milk and took a handful of carrots for the reindeer.

'HO HO HO' said Santa before he disappeared through the front door.

Nilan was still excited about meeting Santa and fell asleep on the sofa thinking about it.

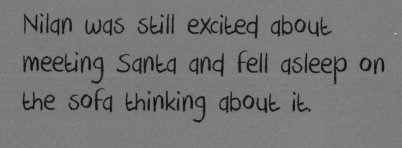

The next morning was
Christmas day.

Nilan's mummy came downstairs and
found Nilan sleeping on the sofa. She
told him off. Nilan told his mummy
that Santa had come to drop off his
present but had gotten stuck in the
chimney and he had helped him out.

Nilan's mummy didn't believe
him and said 'Santa would
have eaten the cookies'.

Nilan smiled to himself again
because he knew the truth.

47346118R00016

Printed in Poland
by Amazon Fulfillment
Poland Sp. z o.o., Wrocław